THE STORY OF THE
OTHER
WISE MAN

THE STORY OF THE
✷ OTHER ✷
WISE MAN

HENRY VAN DYKE

Retold by Michael Lynberg

**Andrews McMeel
Publishing**

Kansas City

00 01 02 03 04 PHX 10 9 8 7 6 5 4 3 2 1

Library of Congress Cataloging-in-Publication Data

Van Dyke, Henry, 1852-1933.
    The story of the other wise man / by Henry Van Dyke ; retold by Michael Lynberg.
        p. cm.
    ISBN 0-7407-1168-7
    1. Jesus Christ—Fiction. 2. Magi—Fiction. I. Lynberg, Michael. II. Title.

PS3117 .S7 2000
813'.52—dc21   00-042136

PREFACE

HE *Story of the Other Wise Man* is considered by many to be one of the greatest Christmas stories ever told. Published in 1895, it was an immediate success and has appeared in a number of editions and translations. Its enduring power lies in its beautiful imagery, rich language, suspenseful story line, and sympathetic characters.

The hero of the story, Artaban, sells all he owns in order to travel with his friends, the other three wise men, to offer gifts to the child Jesus in Bethlehem. Like the other Magi, he has seen the new star, and he knows that he must follow it. But he encounters a number of challenges along the way and gets delayed. *The Story of the Other Wise Man* recounts his remarkable journey.

It is an inspiring tale that enriches all who read it.

The author, Henry Van Dyke, was a man of many talents. While his dream was to be a writer, he attended Princeton Theological Seminary and served for many years as a pastor in Rhode Island and New York. He gained a national reputation for his preaching; *The Story of the Other Wise Man* was originally a Christmas sermon delivered to his New York City congregation. It was so well received that Van Dyke later made it into a book.

In addition to being a talented story-teller and pastor, Van Dyke loved the out-doors and became an ardent conservationist, speaking out for the preservation of Yellow-stone Park, among other places. He was also a prolific literary critic, and in 1900, he became a professor of English literature at Princeton, where he worked for twenty-three years, with some interruptions.

In 1913, his friend and former Princeton classmate, President Woodrow Wilson, appointed Van Dyke United States minister to the Netherlands and Luxembourg. He was serving there when World War I broke out, and because he could not maintain a neutral attitude toward the war—the Netherlands and Luxembourg were neutral—he resigned his post and became a chaplain in the U.S. Naval Reserve. Holding the rank of lieutenant commander, he toured naval

stations and addressed the spiritual needs of military personnel.

Van Dyke received honorary doctor of divinity degrees from Harvard, Princeton, and Yale. In his later years, he tried to counter the cynicism and despair that followed World War I by writing and speaking to audiences across the country; Helen Keller called him an "architect of happiness." He was known for many accomplishments, but *The Story of the Other Wise Man* remains his most beloved work.

For this edition, I have simplified Van Dyke's language and streamlined the story in several places to make it more accessible to a new generation of readers. My goal has been to make it even more of a page-turner, even more visual and cinematic, while remaining true to Van Dyke's original, for the story is entirely his.

I would like to thank Jane Dystel, my literary agent, for working hard to help me achieve my dreams. Thank you also to

Dorothy O'Brien, my editor at Andrews McMeel, for always striving to make a book the best that it can be. And thank you to my wife, Elizabeth, for your constant love and support.

Michael Lynberg
Pacific Grove, California

THE STORY OF THE
OTHER
WISE MAN

OU KNOW THE STORY OF THE THREE wise men of the East, and how they traveled from far away to offer their gifts at the manger-cradle in Bethlehem. But have you ever heard the story of the other wise man, who also saw the star in its rising, and set out to follow it, yet did not arrive

3

with his brethren in the presence of the young child Jesus? Of the great desire of this fourth pilgrim, and how it was denied, yet accomplished in the denial; of his many wanderings and the probations of his soul; of the long way of his seeking, and the strange way of finding, the One whom he sought—I offer this tale.

In the days when Caesar Augustus was master of many kings and Herod reigned in Jerusalem, there lived in the city of Ecbatana, among the mountains of Persia, a certain man named Artaban. He was a tall, dark man of about forty years, with brilliant eyes set near together under his broad brow. His robe was of pure white wool, thrown over a tunic of silk; a white pointed cap, with long lapels at the sides, rested on his flowing black hair. It was the dress of the ancient priesthood of the Magi.

On this night, Artaban welcomed his father and several of his friends to his house near the outermost wall of the city. The men differed widely in age, but they were alike in the richness of their dress of many-colored silks and in the massive golden collars around their necks, marking them as Parthian nobles.

"Welcome!" said Artaban, in his low, pleasant voice, as they entered. "You are all welcome, and my house grows bright with the joy of your presence."

The men sat near a small open fireplace

at the end of a great room. Artaban fed the fire with dry sticks of pine and fragrant oils. The flames illuminated the room, revealing its simplicity and splendor.

"You have come tonight at my call, and I thank you," Artaban said, looking at their faces. "Together, we have searched the secrets of nature, and studied the healing virtues of water and fire and plants. We have read also the books of prophecy in which the future is dimly foretold in words that are hard to understand. Hear me now, my father and my friends, as I tell you of a new light and truth that I feel certain will change our lives.

"You all know of Caspar, Melchior, and Balthazar, three of my companions in the Magi. Their wisdom is unsurpassed; their reputations are beyond reproach. Together, these men and I have searched the ancient tablets, and we have discerned that the time is near for the rising of the God's chosen Redeemer, who will come from the land of

Israel. We have also studied the sky, and in the spring we saw two great planets draw so near together that they became as one, and below them there was a new star that shone for one night and then vanished.

"Tonight, the two planets are meeting again. My three brothers are watching at the ancient temple in Babylonia, and I am watching here. If the star shines again, they will wait ten days for me at the temple, and then we will set out together for Jerusalem, to see and worship the Promised One who shall be born the King of Israel. I believe the sign will come. I have made ready for the journey. I have sold my house and my possessions, and bought these three jewels—a sapphire, a ruby, and a pearl—to carry them as tribute to the King. I ask you to go with me on the pilgrimage, that we may have joy together in finding the Prince who is worthy to be served."

While he was speaking he drew from his pocket three great gems—one blue as a fragment of the night sky, one redder than a ray of light at sunrise, and one as pure as the peak of a snow mountain at twilight—and laid them out before him.

But his friends looked on with strange and alien eyes. A veil of doubt and mistrust came over their faces. They glanced at each other with looks of wonder and pity, as those who have listened to incredible sayings, the story of a wild vision, or the proposal of an impossible enterprise.

At last one of them said, "Artaban, this is a vain dream. It comes from too much looking at the stars and the cherishing of lofty thoughts. No king will ever rise from the broken race of Israel, and no end will ever come to the eternal strife of light and darkness. He who looks for it is a chaser of shadows. Farewell."

And another said, "Artaban, I have no knowledge of these things, and my office as guardian of the royal treasure binds me here.

The quest is not for me. But if you must follow it, then God be with you."

And another said, "In my house there sleeps a new bride, and I cannot leave her nor take her with me on this strange journey. This quest is not for me. But may your steps be prospered wherever you go. So farewell."

But Artaban's father, the oldest and the one who loved him the best, lingered after the others had gone. Gravely he said, "My son, it may be that the light of truth is in this sign that has appeared in the skies, and then it will surely lead to the Prince and eternal truth. Or maybe it is only a shadow of the light, and then he who follows it will have only a long pilgrimage and an empty search. But you must be true to your calling. And those who would see and do wonderful things must often be ready to travel alone. I am too old for this journey, but my heart will be your companion day and night. Go in peace."

So one by one they went out, and
Artaban was left in solitude. He gathered up
the jewels and put them back in his pocket.
For a long time he stood and watched the
flame that flickered in the fireplace. Then he
crossed the room and went out to a terrace
on the roof.

Morning was near, and a cool wind blew
down from the lofty snow-traced ravines of
Mount Orontes. Birds, half awakened, crept
and chirped among the rustling leaves, and

the smell of ripened grapes came in brief wafts from the arbors in Artaban's garden.

Far over the eastern plain a white mist stretched like a lake. But where the distant mountain peaks serrated the western horizon, the sky was clear. Jupiter and Saturn rolled together like drops of lambent flame about to blend into one.

As Artaban watched them, behold! a spark emerged from the darkness beneath. It rose to a point of white radiance in the sky, emanating rays of purple, crimson, saffron, and orange. Tiny and infinitely remote, yet perfect in every part, it pulsated as if the three jewels in the Magian's breast had mingled and been transformed into a living heart of light.

He bowed his head and covered his brow with his hands.

"It is the sign," he said. "The King is coming, and I will go to meet Him."

BY THE
WATERS
OF
BABYLON

ALL NIGHT LONG VASDA, THE SWIFTEST of Artaban's horses, had been waiting, saddled and bridled, in her stall, pawing the ground impatiently and shaking her bit as if she shared the eagerness of her master's purpose, though she knew not its meaning.

Before the birds had fully roused to their strong, high, joyful chant of morning song, before the white mist had begun to lift lazily from the plain, the other wise man was in the saddle, riding swiftly along the high road, which skirted the base of Mount Orontes, westward.

How close, how intimate is the comradeship between a man and his favorite horse on a long journey. It is a silent, comprehensive friendship, beyond the need of words. They drink at the same wayside spring, share their evening meal, and sleep under the same guardian stars. The man is awakened from his sleep by the gentle stirring of his faithful fellow traveler, who stands ready and waiting for the toil of the day. Surely, unless he is a pagan and an unbeliever, by whatever name he calls upon his God, he will thank Him for this voiceless sympathy, this dumb affection, and his morning prayer will embrace a double blessing—God bless us both, and keep our feet from falling and our bodies from death!

And then, through the keen morning air, the swift hoofs beat their spirited music along the road, keeping time to the pulsing of two hearts that are moved with the same eager desire—to conquer space, to devour the distance, to attain the goal of the journey.

Artaban knew that he must ride wisely and well if he would keep the appointed hour with the other Magi; for the route was 150 parasangs, and fifteen was the utmost that he could travel in a day. He had confidence in Vasda's strength, and pushed forward without anxiety, making the fixed distance every day, though he had to travel late into the night, and in the morning long before sunrise.

He passed along the brown slopes of Mount Orontes, furrowed by the rocky courses of a hundred torrents.

He made his way through verdant meadows, where herds of wild horses, feeding in the pastures, tossed their heads at Vasda's approach and galloped away with a thunder of many hoofs.

He passed through groves of peach and fig trees, where flocks of birds rose suddenly from the high branches, wheeling in great circles with a shining flutter of innumerable wings and shrill cries of surprise.

He crossed many a cold and desolate pass, crawling painfully along the windswept shoulders of the hills, and down many a black mountain gorge, where the river roared and raced before him like a savage guide.

He continued over the flat plains, where the road ran straight as an arrow through stubble fields and parched meadows, pointing toward his destiny.

On the tenth day, as they approached the shattered walls of populous Babylon, Vasda was almost spent. Artaban would gladly have turned into the city to find rest and refreshment for himself and for her, but he knew that it was three hours' journey yet to the temple. He had to reach the place by midnight if he would find his companions waiting. So he did not halt, but rode steadily onward.

In the darkness, on a path lined with palm trees, Vasda slackened her pace and began to pick her way more carefully. She scented some danger or difficulty. It was not in her nature to fly from it—only to be prepared, and meet it wisely. The night was silent as a tomb; not a leaf rustled, not a bird sang.

She felt her steps before her delicately, carrying her head low, and sighing now and then with apprehension. At last she gave a quick breath of anxiety and dismay, and stood quivering in every muscle, before a dark object in the shadow of the last palm tree.

Artaban dismounted. The dim starlight revealed the form of a man lying across the road. His humble dress and the outline of his haggard face showed that he was probably one of the poor Hebrew exiles who dwelt in great numbers in the vicinity. His pallid skin, dry and yellow as parchment, bore the mark of a deadly fever that often ravaged the marshlands in autumn. The chill of death was in his lean hand, and, as Artaban released it, the man's arm fell back inertly upon his motionless breast.

Artaban uttered a prayer for the man's eternal soul and vowed to find someone in the next village to give him a proper burial.

But, as he turned away, in a rush to meet

his friends, a long, faint, ghostly sigh came from the man's lips. The brown, bony fingers closed convulsively on the hem of the Magian's robe and held him fast.

Artaban's heart leaped to his throat, not with fear, but with resentment for the importunity of this blind delay.

How could he stay here in the darkness to minister to a dying stranger? What claim had this unknown fragment of human life upon his compassion or his service? If he

lingered but for an hour, he could hardly
reach the temple at the appointed time. His
companions would think he had given up
the journey. They would go without him.
He would lose his quest. But if he left, the
man would surely die. Artaban's spirit
throbbed and fluttered with the urgency of
the crisis. Should he risk the great reward of
his faith for the sake of a single deed of
human love? Should he turn aside, if only for
a moment, from following the star, to give a

cup of cold water to a poor, perishing man?

"God of truth and purity," he prayed, "direct me in the way of wisdom, which only you can know."

Then he turned back to the sick man. Loosening the grasp of his hand, he carried him to a little mound at the foot of the palm tree.

He unbound the thick folds of the turban and opened the garment above the sunken breast. He brought water from a nearby stream, and moistened the sufferer's brow and mouth. He mingled a draught of one of those simple but potent remedies that he carried always with him—for the Magians were also physicians—and poured it slowly between the colorless lips. Hour after hour, he labored as only a skillful healer of disease can do. At last, the man's strength returned; he sat up and looked about him.

"Who are you?" he asked, in weak and raspy voice.

"I am Artaban the Magian, of the city of Ecbatana, and I am going to Jerusalem in search of One who is to be born King of the Jews, a great Prince and Savior. I dare not delay any longer, for the caravan that has waited for me may depart without me. But see, here is all that I have left of bread and wine, and here is a potion of healing herbs. When your strength is restored you can find the dwellings of the Hebrews among the houses of Babylon."

The man raised his trembling hand
solemnly to heaven. "Go, please! You have
done enough. May the God of Abraham and
Isaac and Jacob bless and prosper your journey, and bring you in peace to your desired
haven. I have nothing to give you in return for
saving my life—only this: I can tell you where
the Messiah must be sought. For our prophets
have said that He should be born not in
Jerusalem, but in Bethlehem of Judah. May
the Lord bring you in safety to that place."

It was already long past midnight. Artaban rode in haste, and Vasda, restored by the brief rest, ran eagerly through the silent plain and swam the channels of the river. She put forth the remnant of her strength, galloping at a thunderous clip.

As the first beams of sunlight sent her shadow before her, Vasda entered upon the final stretch of the journey. Artaban anxiously scanned the temple grounds, looking for his friends. He could see no trace of them.

He rode to a high place where he could look out toward the western horizon; still, there was no sign of the wise men or their caravan, near or far.

Returning to the front of the temple, he saw a little cairn of broken bricks, and under them a piece of parchment. He lifted it up and read, "We have waited past midnight and can delay no longer. We go to find the King. Follow us across the desert."

Artaban sat down upon the ground and covered his head in despair.

"How can I cross the desert," he said, "with no food and a spent horse? I must return to Babylon, sell my sapphire, and buy a train of camels and provisions for the journey. I may never catch up to my friends. Only God the merciful knows whether I shall not lose sight of the King because I tarried to show mercy."

FOR THE
SAKE
OF A
LITTLE
CHILD

RTABAN SOLD THE SAPPHIRE, BOUGHT the necessary supplies, and set out across the desert. Sitting high upon the back of his camel, he rocked steadily onward, like a ship over the waves.

The land of death spread its cruel net around him. Shifting hills of sand stretched as far as the eye could see, and the wind stung his face. The arid landscape bore no fruit but briers and thorns. Days of fierce heat were followed by nights of bitter cold. Through it all, the Magian pressed onward, guided by the distant star.

Parched and weary but full of hope and bearing his gifts for the King, he made it through the desert to the gardens and orchards of Damascus, watered by a myriad of streams. Pausing only briefly for more provisions, he continued on to the valley of the Jordan, past the blue waters of the Sea of Galilee, and across the highlands of Judah. Finally, he arrived in Bethlehem.

The streets of the village seemed to be deserted, and Artaban wondered whether the men had all gone up to the hill pastures to bring down their sheep. Then he heard the sound of a woman singing softly, and he saw a soft light coming from the window of a small stone cottage. He knocked on the door and the woman opened it up. She was holding a baby and trying to comfort the child to sleep.

Artaban quietly told her why he was there and asked if she had seen his friends. She asked him to step inside and said, "Yes, they were here. It is not every day that we see travelers from such distant lands. They said that they had followed a star to the place where a man from Nazareth, named Joseph, was resting with his wife, Mary, and her newborn son.

"They brought the child rich gifts of gold and frankincense and myrrh, but then they disappeared, as suddenly as they had come. We were afraid at the strangeness of their visit. We could not understand it. The man of Nazareth took the baby and his mother and fled away that same night secretly, and it was whispered that they were going far away to Egypt. Ever since there has been a spell upon the village; something evil hangs over it. They say that the Roman soldiers are

coming from Jerusalem to force a new tax
from us, and the men have driven the flocks
and herds far back among the hills, and
hidden themselves to escape it."

Artaban listened to her gentle speech
and the child in her arms looked up and
smiled at him, stretching out a tiny hand to
touch his weathered face. His heart warmed
to the touch. It seemed like a greeting of
love and trust to one who had journeyed so
far in loneliness and perplexity, fighting with

his own doubts and fears, and following a light that sometimes was veiled in clouds.

"Might not this child have been the Promised One?" he asked within himself, as he looked upon the baby. "Kings have been born in lowlier houses than this, and the favorite of the heavens may rise even from a cottage. But it has not seemed good to the God of Wisdom to reward my search so soon and so easily. The One whom I seek has gone before me; and now I must follow Him to Egypt."

The young mother laid the baby in a cradle, and insisted that Artaban have something to eat. She set the food before him. It was the plain fare of peasants, but willingly offered, and therefore full of refreshment for the soul as well as for the body. Artaban was grateful, and as he ate the baby fell into a happy slumber, murmuring sweetly, and a great peace filled the quiet room.

But suddenly there came the noise of a wild confusion and uproar in the streets of the village, a shrieking and wailing of women's voices, a clangor of swords, and a desperate cry: "The soldiers! The soldiers of Herod! They are killing our children!"

The young mother's face grew white with terror. She clasped her child to her bosom, and crouched motionless in the darkest corner of the room, covering him with the folds of her robe, lest he should wake and cry. Artaban went quickly and stood in the doorway, his broad shoulders filling the entry from side to side.

The soldiers came hurrying down the street with bloody hands and dripping swords. At the sight of the stranger in his imposing dress they hesitated with surprise. The captain of the band approached the threshold to thrust him aside. But Artaban did not stir. His face was as calm as though he were watching the stars, and in his eyes there burned that steady radiance that would keep even a vicious dog in its place. He held the soldier silently for an instant, and then said, in a low voice,

"I am all alone in this place, and I am waiting to give this jewel to the prudent captain who will leave me in peace."

He showed the ruby, glistening in the hollow of his hand like a great drop of blood.

The captain was amazed at the splendor of the gem. The pupils of his eyes expanded with desire, and the hard lines of greed wrinkled around his lips. He stretched out his hand and took the ruby.

"March on!" he cried to his men. "There is no child here. The house is still."

The clamor and the clang of arms passed down the street. Artaban re-entered the cottage and fell to his knees.

"God, forgive me!" he said. "I have told a lie, and two of my gifts are gone. I have spent for man that which was meant for God. Shall I ever be worthy to see the face of the King?"

But the woman, weeping in gratitude and still trembling with fear, said through her tears: "You have saved the life of my child. May the Lord bless you and keep you. May He make His face to shine upon you. May He be gracious to you and give you peace."

IN THE
HIDDEN
WAY
OF
SORROW

ND SO ARTABAN TRAVELED FIRST TO Egypt and then to other places, looking for the family that had fled from Bethlehem. At times he got close, but he was always one step behind them. Their traces vanished before him, as footprints glisten and disappear on the hard river sand.

Weeks and months passed, and Artaban visited the house of a rabbi. The venerable man, bending over the rolls of parchment on which the prophecies of Israel were written, read aloud the words that foretold the sufferings of the promised Messiah—the despised and rejected of men, the man of sorrows and the acquaintance of grief.

"Remember, my son," he said, fixing his eyes upon the face of Artaban, "the King whom you are seeking is not to be found in a palace, nor among the rich and powerful. If the light of the world and the glory of Israel had been appointed to come with the greatness of earthly splendor, it must have appeared long ago. For no son of Abraham will ever again rival the power that Joseph had in Egypt, or the magnificence of Solomon in Jerusalem. But the light for which the world is waiting is a new light, the glory that shall rise out of patient and triumphant suffering. And the kingdom that is to be established forever is a new kingdom of perfect and unconquerable love.

"I do not know how this shall come to pass, nor how the turbulent kingdoms and peoples of earth shall be brought to acknowledge the Messiah and pay homage to Him. But this I know. Those who seek Him will do well to look among the poor and oppressed, the sorrowful and the lonely."

So the other wise man traveled near and far, again and again, looking for the family from Bethlehem. He passed through countries where famine lay heavy upon the land and the poor were crying for bread. He made his dwelling in plague-stricken cities where the sick were languishing in the bitter companionship of helpless misery. He visited the oppressed and the afflicted in the gloom of subterranean prisons and the crowded wretchedness of slave markets and the weary toil of galley ships. In all this populous and intricate world of anguish, though he found none to worship, he found many to help. He fed the hungry and clothed the naked and healed the sick and comforted the captive. But he was never able to find and worship the Messiah whom he sought.

Once, while standing alone at the gate of a Roman prison, Artaban took the last of his gifts from its secret place in his garment. The pearl looked soft and mellow in the morning light. It seemed to have absorbed some of the colors of the sapphire and ruby, much as a noble life absorbs and reflects its past joys and sorrows. Artaban carefully put it back in his pocket, near his heart.

A
PEARL
OF
GREAT
PRICE

HIRTY-THREE YEARS PASSED AWAY, and Artaban still searched. His hair, once dark, was now white as snow. His eyes, once bright, were now dull and tired.

Worn and weary and ready to die, but still looking for the King, he had come for the last time to Jerusalem. He had visited the

holy city before and had searched through all its lanes and crowded hovels and dark prisons without finding any trace of the family who had fled from Bethlehem long ago. But now it seemed as if he must make one more effort, and something whispered in his heart that, at last, he might succeed.

It was the season of the Passover. The city was thronged with people. The children of Israel, scattered all over the world, had returned to the temple for the great feast, and there had been a confusion of tongues in the narrow streets for many days.

But on this day there was a singular agitation visible in the multitude. The sky was veiled with a portentous gloom, and currents of excitement seemed to flash through the crowd like the thrill that shakes a forest on the eve of a storm. A secret tide was sweeping them all one way. The clatter of sandals filled the air as the crowd flowed unceasingly along the street that led to the Damascus gate.

Artaban joined a group of people from his own country, Parthian Jews who had come to keep the Passover, and asked them about the cause of the tumult, and where they were going.

"Have you not heard what has happened?" they answered. Two famous robbers are to be crucified, and with them another, called Jesus of Nazareth, a man who has done many wonderful works among the people, so that they love him greatly. But the priests and elders have said that he must die, because he gave himself out to be the Son of God. And Pilate has sent him to the cross because he said that he was the 'King of the Jews.' We are going to the place called Golgotha, outside the city walls, where the execution will take place."

How strangely these familiar words fell upon the tired heart of Artaban! The King had arisen, but He had been denied and cast out. He was about to perish. Perhaps He was already dying. Could it be the same who had been born in Bethlehem thirty-three years ago, at whose birth the star had appeared in heaven, and of whose coming the prophets had spoken?

Artaban's heart beat unsteadily, and he said to himself: "The ways of God are mysterious, and it may be that I shall find the King, at last, in the hands of His enemies, and shall come in time to offer my pearl for His ransom before He dies."

So the old man followed the multitude with slow and painful steps toward the Damascus gate. As they made their way, a troop of Macedonian soldiers came down the street, dragging a young woman with a torn dress and disheveled hair. She was crying desperately, and as the Magian paused to look at her with compassion, she broke free from her tormentors and threw herself at his feet.

"Have pity on me," she cried. "My father

has died, and I am being sold as a slave to pay for his debts. Please save me from a fate worse than death!"

Artaban trembled. It was the old conflict in his soul, which had come to him in the palm grove of Babylon and in the cottage in Bethlehem—the conflict between the expectation of faith and the impulse of love. Twice the gift that he had consecrated to the worship of religion had been drawn from his hand to the service of humanity.

This was the third trial, the ultimate probation, the final and irrevocable choice.

Was it his great opportunity, or his last temptation? He could not tell. One thing only was clear in the confusion of his mind—it was inevitable. And does not the inevitable come from God? One thing only was sure to his divided heart—to rescue this helpless girl would be an act of love. And is not love the light of the soul?

He took the pearl from his pocket.

Never had it seemed so luminous, so radiant, so full of tender, living luster. He laid it in the hand of the slave.

"This is your ransom, daughter! It is the last of my treasures that I kept for the King."

While he spoke, the darkness of the sky thickened, and shuddering tremors ran through the earth, heaving convulsively like the breast of one who struggles with mighty grief.

The walls of buildings rocked to and fro. Stones were loosened and crashed into the street. Dust clouds filled the air. The soldiers fled in terror, reeling like drunken men. But Artaban and the girl whom he had ransomed took shelter next to a house.

What had he to fear? What had he to live for? He had given away the last remnant of his tribute for the King. He had parted with the last hope of finding Him. The quest was over, and it had failed. But, even in that thought, accepted and embraced, there was peace. It was not resignation. It was not

submission. It was something more pro-
found and searching. He knew that all was
well, because he had done the best that he
could, from day to day. He had been true to
the light that had been given to him.

One more lingering pulsation of the
earthquake quivered through the ground.
A heavy tile, shaken from a roof above, fell
and struck Artaban on the temple. He lay
breathless and pale, cradled in the young
woman's arms, blood trickling from the

wound. As she bent over him, fearing that he was dead, there came a voice through the twilight, very small and still, like music sounding from a distance, in which the notes are clear but the words are lost. The girl turned to see if someone had spoken from the window above them, but she saw no one.

Then the old man's lips began to move, as if in answer, and she heard him say, "Not so, my Lord: For when did I see you hungry and feed you? Or thirsty, and give you drink? When did I see you as a stranger, and take you in? Or naked, and clothe you? When did I see you sick or in prison, and visit you? For three and thirty years I have looked for you, but I have never seen your face, nor ministered to you, my King."

He ceased, and the sweet voice came again. And again the girl heard it, very faintly and far away. But now it seemed as though she understood the words.

"I tell you the truth, whatever you did
for one of the least of these brothers of mine,
you did for me."

A calm radiance of wonder and joy lighted the pale face of Artaban like the first ray of dawn on a snowy mountain peak. One long, last breath came gently from his lips.

His journey was ended. His treasures were accepted. The other wise man had found the King.